EASTER
PARADE

EASTER PARADE

Eloise Greenfield

ILLUSTRATED BY JAN SPIVEY GILCHRIST

Hyperion Books for Children
New York

Printed in Singapore.

First Edition
1 3 5 7 9 10 8 6 4 2

The artwork for each picture is prepared using graphite.
This book is set in 14-point BeLucian.

Library of Congress Cataloging-in-Publication Data

Greenfield, Eloise
Easter Parade / Eloise Greenfield ; illustrated by Jan Spivey Gilchrist.
p.   cm.
Summary: Although the young cousins live many miles apart, Leanna in Chicago
and Elizabeth in Washington, D.C., both prepare for an Easter parade against the
backdrop of the Second World War.
ISBN 0-7868-0326-6 (trade)—ISBN 0-7868-2271-6 (lib. bdg.)
[1. Easter—Fiction. 2. Parades—Fiction. 3. Cousins—Fiction. 4. Afro-
Americans—Fiction. 5. United States—History—1939-1945—Fiction.] I. Gilchrist,
Jan Spivey, ill. II. Title.
PZ7.G845Eas   1997
[E]—dc21   97-14279

To the memory of Mama and Daddy
—E. G.

For Aunt Sular
Thanks for the memories and all of the love
—J. S. G.

CHAPTER ONE

*I*t is the year 1943, and in a pale-yellow frame house on a long street in the city of Chicago, Leanna sits on the floor, playing with her doll and listening to the fast clicking sounds of the sewing machine. *Click-click, click-click, click-click, click-click.* Her mother is sewing, making a dress for Mrs. Banks, touching the cloth lightly, helping it to glide along under the needle that goes up and down and up and down.

Leanna holds in both hands a little piece of the pretty cloth, a piece her mother doesn't need. It is thin and soft, soft like the doll, and Leanna loves the way it feels. She smooths it out and wraps it around her

doll like a baby's blanket. She holds the doll in one arm and pats her with the other hand, the way she has seen Mrs. Marshall, her next-door neighbor, pat her new baby.

Leanna's mother cuts the threads, puts the cloth aside, and places another piece under the needle. She speaks without turning away from the machine.

"The days are flying," she says. "I've got to get started on *your* dress in a day or two. It's almost time for the Easter parade."

"What's the Easter parade?" Leanna asks.

"Remember last year?" Mama says. "Remember?"

Leanna lays her doll on the carpet and gives her one last pat to put her to sleep.

3

"No," she says. "I don't remember that, Mama."

Her mother begins to tell her about it, but Leanna forgets to listen. She is thinking about the word "parade," saying it over and over in her mind. She likes the way it sounds. She takes it apart, "puh-rade," and puts it back together again, "parade, parade."

Pictures begin to slide through her mind, one after the other, slowly. She sees a picture of herself walking, and her daddy holding her hand, and her big brother, Raymond, walking beside them. She sees a crowd of people, other children and grown-ups, and more children and more grown-ups, walking. She sees herself in Daddy's arms, and all the people

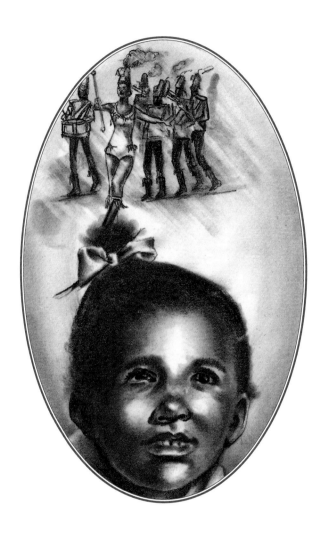

stopping and leaning over and looking way down the street, waiting for something.

The pictures in her mind move faster, their colors racing by. Two women are marching, stepping high, spinning their batons into the air and catching them when they fall. A marching man pounds on the big drum he carries on his stomach. A group of men, a group of women, march by blowing horns, waving them left and right, left and right, in time with the music. The people watching are clapping and pointing, and, in her daddy's arms, Leanna is clapping, too.

Over the faraway clicking of the sewing machine, Leanna hears her mother's laughter, and the pictures disappear.

"Leanna," her mother says, "am I talking to myself again? You haven't heard a word I've said."

"I know what the parade is, Mama," Leanna says. "It has marching. And horns and drums."

"You're right," her mother says. "That's one kind of parade. But this parade is different. Wait until Easter Sunday. You'll see."

"Can Elizabeth come to visit, so she can see it, too?"

"Oh, Elizabeth is going to see a parade right there where she lives," her mother says.

"Can I call and tell her?"

"I think she knows it."

"But can I call her?"

"Right now?"

"Can I?"

Her mother sighs loudly, joking. "Come on," she says.

At the telephone table, Leanna sits the way she has seen her mother sit. She crosses her legs and picks up the phone. A woman's voice, almost singing, says, "Operator."

"I want long distance, please, Operator," Leanna says. "I want to call somebody in Washington, D.C." She looks at her mother to see if she has said it right. Her mother nods yes, bends toward the receiver, and gives the operator Elizabeth's number. Leanna hears the telephone ringing at Elizabeth's house.

CHAPTER TWO

*I*n a red-brick rowhouse on a long
street in Washington, D.C., Elizabeth
hears the phone, but she doesn't look at it.
She looks at her mother. Her mother's
eyes are frightened.

Elizabeth's fingers tighten around the
picture she is holding in her lap, a picture

of her father in his Army uniform. He is far away, fighting in the war. She and her mother have been talking about missing him, and about his letters that used to come almost every day and now have stopped coming. They have been telling each other that he is all right, that no one will call on the phone to say that he has been hurt.

Her mother catches a breath and reaches for the phone.

"Hello?" she says. Her voice trembles. She listens, then smiles and speaks to Leanna.

"Hi, baby," she says. "How are you?" She listens again, then says, "That's good. Okay, here she is." She hands the phone to Elizabeth.

"Hi, Leanna," Elizabeth says.

"Do you know about the parade?" Leanna asks.

"What parade?"

"The Easter parade!" Leanna says. "You're going to have one, and I'm going to have one, too."

"Oh, I know," Elizabeth says. She tries to sound excited to make her little cousin

happy. "It's going to be fun."

"Mama's going to sew me a new dress so I can go to it," Leanna says. "You going to it?"

"I think so," Elizabeth says.

"Okay. Guess what, I know a new joke!" Leanna says. "You want to hear it?"

Leanna starts one of her too-long

jokes, making it up as she goes along, and Elizabeth gets tickled and really laughs. She forgets about her worry. When she hands the phone to her mother, she is still laughing.

She watches as her mother talks to Leanna's mother, two sisters who love each other.

"No," her mother is saying, "no letter yet. It's been more than three weeks now."

She puts her mouth close to the phone and talks so quietly that Elizabeth can't understand the words. Then her mother stops talking and listens, and her eyes are shiny with tears.

"You're right," she says. "A letter will come. Maybe tomorrow." In a few moments, she is laughing, her eyes

still wet. Her sister has said something funny.

When she hangs up the phone, she turns to look at Elizabeth. She asks a question with her eyes. "Do we want to have Easter?" her eyes say.

"I think Daddy wants us to," Elizabeth says.

Her mother nods. "We can't buy new clothes this year, you know. We've been sending money to Grandma."

"I know," Elizabeth says. "That's okay."

CHAPTER THREE

The days pass, and two families get ready for the Easter parade.

In Chicago, Leanna's father and brother go shopping together, and Leanna goes shopping with her mother. She walks down the aisle of the fabric store, looking at large rolls of cloth. When

 19

she sees a color she likes, she stops and rubs the cloth gently with the tips of her fingers to see if it feels special.

"The yellow one," she says, sliding her hand across the cloth that is slippery and bright. "I want the yellow one."

Her mother will make it into a dress with coat to match.

At the shoe store Leanna tries on three pairs of shoes, all of them made of black patent leather. They are glossy, almost like dark mirrors, reflecting the lights in the store. Leanna chooses the shoes with the T-strap, the strap that comes down the middle of her foot.

At the department store, she picks out a black patent leather pocketbook with a gold chain, white cotton gloves, yellow

ankle-socks trimmed with white lace, and a straw hat with a turned-up brim and yellow ribbon that winds around and hangs down the back.

In Washington, D.C., Elizabeth's god-mother comes to visit, bringing black patent leather shoes and two dresses that her daughter has outgrown. Elizabeth

tries on the shoes. They are only a little scuffed. Her mother mashes the toes to be sure they fit. She will oil them with petroleum jelly and make them shine like new.

Elizabeth spreads the two dresses out on the bed, trying to decide which one will be her Easter dress. She chooses the one that is blue. She puts it on and twirls. The dress swirls around her, making blue streaks in the air. In the mirror, she sees her mother and godmother smiling at her. She smiles at herself and pretends that her father is there saying "*beautiful* girl, *beautiful* girl" in his usual way.

Every afternoon now, Elizabeth and her mother stand at the window and wait

 23

for the mailman, and every day, they are disappointed. As soon as they see the mailman's face, they know he doesn't have the letter they want. His face is tight and closed. It's not the face he used to have. He knows he is bringing them bad news.

On the day before Easter, Elizabeth's

mother doesn't go to the window. "We
don't need to be there," she says. "Mr.
Anderson will put the mail in the box.
Let's do something else."

But Elizabeth wants to be there. She
sits on the arm of the stuffed chair and
presses her elbows stiffly against her sides,
getting herself ready for disappointment.
She sees the mailman coming toward the
house. He is taking long steps. His face is
smooth and happy.

"Mama?" Elizabeth says, much too
softly for her mother to hear. She thinks
this face is just her wish, that she has only
imagined it. She is afraid to hope. She
watches Mr. Anderson reach into his
leather bag and pull out two letters. He
holds them up and waves them at her.

"*Mama!*" Elizabeth screams. "*Mama!*"

The mailman leaves the letters, one for her mother and one for her, along with a package for Elizabeth from Chicago. Elizabeth puts the package aside and hands a letter to her mother. She sits across the room from her mother, facing away from her. She wants to be alone and try to hear her father's voice. The letter says:

> *Dear Elizabeth,*
> *I want you to know that I'm all right. I've been in a place where I could not write to you, but I'm in a good place now. I think of you and your mother every minute. Every minute. I love you.*
> *Daddy*

"Is he coming home soon?" she asks her mother.

"He didn't say," her mother answers. "He's very tired. But he's safe. *Ohhh, he's safe*," she says again and starts to cry. She walks quickly from the room.

Elizabeth doesn't move. She sits and listens to the sobs coming from her mother's bedroom. Then she reaches for the package she has forgotten until now and slowly opens it. It's a present from Leanna, a black patent leather pocketbook with a thin matching strap. Elizabeth opens it and puts her letter inside.

CHAPTER FOUR

That night, in two cities, two mothers are combing their daughters' hair, parting it into small sections and rolling it up on curlers. Later, two daughters lay their heads carefully on their pillows and daydream, for just a little while, before they close their eyes and go to sleep.

Now it is morning. Easter Sunday morning in the month of April, in the year 1943. In Washington, D.C., Elizabeth and her mother, dressed in their Easter clothes, are seated in church.

From her seat near the middle of the church, Elizabeth can see rows of colorful spring hats worn by the women and girls. Straw hats decorated with ribbons and flowers, some of them covered with puffs of veil.

Elizabeth bows her head as the minister starts to pray. She lets herself feel his quiet words and the comfort of knowing that her father is all right. She feels the beauty of this day and she is happy. But inside the happiness, there is a sharp sadness because her father is not there.

She leans against her mother and her mother puts her arm around her. Elizabeth prays that her father will soon be home.

After the service, she and her mother ride on a streetcar crowded with people on their way to the parade. They get off at the corner of Twelfth and U Streets.

There are people already there, some of them just standing and watching, admiring those who are strolling up and down the street. "You are *so* pretty!" they tell the girls. "You are *some* kind of handsome!" they tell the boys.

For a few moments, Elizabeth and her mother stand with the watchers. Then, holding hands, they step into the Easter parade and walk slowly down U Street.

In Chicago, it has rained on Easter Sunday morning, and the sky is still gray, but the rain has stopped, at least for a little while. Leanna, waiting near the door, is dressed up in her Easter dress and her Easter coat and hat and shoes and socks and gloves.

She shakes her pocketbook to hear the jingle of the nickel and two pennies that she will put in the church basket.

She is ready to go. *Everybody* is ready to go, except her brother, who is standing in front of the full-length mirror again.

"Raymond, come on!" she says. She has been waiting too many days to find out what this parade is all about. A different kind of parade. No drums, no marching, no spinning batons. And today they will *walk* to church instead of taking the car.

Outside, Leanna and Raymond walk in front, their parents behind. Leanna looks back at her parents, knowing they will be walking close together, her mother's arm looped through her father's. She smiles her excitement at her parents.

"Happy Easter!" a neighbor calls, and Leanna answers.

"Happy Easter to you!" she says.

Today, there are more people out than usual, heading for their churches. The men nod their heads slightly as they pass, touching the brims of their hats, thumb on the bottom, two curved fingers on top. The boys, dressed like their fathers, have a new, serious walk.

Leanna looks up the street and down the street, trying to find the big parade. The closer she gets to the church, the more people there are. Now they are coming from all directions, moving toward the gray stone building with the sign in the window.

And then she sees the parade, she sees it. It's all around her, and she is *in* it. She's *in* the parade. She feels the rippling motion of many people walking. She sees the many colors of dresses and coats, and hats with flowers, and hats with ribbons that flutter softly as the girls turn their heads. She hears the rhythms of shoe heels hitting the sidewalk like muted drums. She hears the music in the voices, high and low and in-between, saying, "Happy Easter. Happy Easter. Happy Easter."

A little way down the street, her friends are standing in front of the church, but Leanna doesn't run to meet them. And doesn't call. And doesn't wave. She's

 39

in the parade. She feels herself moving with the rhythms. Herself. Mama Daddy Raymond. All the people. Moving. She's in the parade. She's in the parade. Parade. Puh-rade. *Easter parade.*

ABOUT
EASTER PARADE

I was almost fourteen when Easter came in A[pril]
1943, but I don't remember that particular day. T[he]
Easters of my childhood are pieces of mem[ory]
that come and go, undated. I'm little, I'm big. Ma[ma]
and Daddy are always there. Other family, [too]
sometimes, and friends. I'm in Sunday School. I'm [on]
U Street, watching the parade. I'm walking in [the]
grass near the river. The sun is shining. I feel pr[oud]
standing under the cherry blossoms in the dress [that]
Mama has made.

—E. G.

Petticoats and clicking heels, spinning white rib[bons]
on bonnets fly, and Mama strutting down the ch[urch]
aisle showing off her little chicks, . . . that was E[aster]
Sunday.

—J. S. G.